What Kids Say About Carole Marsh Mysteries...

I love the real locations! Reading the book always makes me want to go and visit them all on our next family vacation. My Mom says maybe, but I can't wait!

One day, I want to be a real kid in one of Ms. Marsh's mystery books. I think it would be fun, and I think I am a real character anyway. I filled out the application and sent it in and am keeping my fingers crossed!

History was not my favorite subject until I starting reading Carole Marsh Mysteries. Ms. Marsh really brings history to life. Also, she leaves room for the scary and fun.

I think Christina is so smart and brave. She is lucky to be in the mystery books because she gets to go to a lot of places. I always wonder just how much of the book is true and what is made up. Trying to figure that out is fun!

Grant is cool and funny! He makes me laugh a lot!!

I like that there are boys and girls in the story of different ages. Some mysteries I outgrow, but I can always find a favorite character to identify with in these books.

They are scary, but not too scary. They are funny. I learn a lot. There is always food which makes me hungry. I feel like I am there.

What Parents and Teachers Say About Carole Marsh Mysteries . . .

I think kids love these books because they have such a wealth of detail. I know I learn a lot reading them! It's an engaging way to look at the history of any place or event. I always say I'm only going to read one chapter to the kids, but that never happens—it's always two or three, at least!
—Librarian

Reading the mystery and going on the field trip—Scavenger Hunt in hand—was the most fun our class ever had! It really brought the place and its history to life. They loved the real kids characters and all the humor. I loved seeing them learn that reading is an experience to enjoy! —4th grade teacher

Carole Marsh is really on to something with these unique mysteries. They are so clever; kids want to read them all. The Teacher's Guides are chock full of activities, recipes, and additional fascinating information. My kids thought I was an expert on the subject—and with this tool, I felt like it!
—3rd grade teacher

My students loved writing their own mystery book!
Ms. Marsh's reproducible guidelines are a real jewel. They learned about copyright and ended up with their own book they were so proud of!
—Reading/Writing Teacher

"The kids seem very realistic—my children seemed to relate to the characters. Also, it is educational by expanding their knowledge about the famous places in the books."

"They are what children like: mysteries and adventures with children they can relate to."

"Encourages reading for pleasure."

"This series is great. It can be used for reluctant readers, and as a history supplement."

MASTERS OF DISASTERS

THE FEROCIOUS FOREST FIRE MYSTERY

By
Carole Marsh

Published by Gallopade International/Carole Marsh Books. Printed in the United States of America.

Managing Editor: Sherry Moss
Senior Editor: Janice Baker
Assistant Editor: Mike Kelly
Cover Design & Illustrations: John Kovaleski (www.kovaleski.com)
Content Design: Darryl Lilly, Outreach Graphics

Gallopade International is introducing SAT words that kids need to know in each new book that we publish. The SAT words are bold in the story. Look for this special logo beside each word in the glossary. Happy Learning!

Gallopade is proud to be a member and supporter of these educational organizations and associations:

American Booksellers Association

American Library Association

International Reading Association

National Association for Gifted Children

The National School Supply and Equipment Association

The National Council for the Social Studies

Museum Store Association

Association of Partners for Public Lands

Association of Booksellers for Children

A Word from the Author

What is more frightening than fire? I believe in stop/drop/and roll! I believe in smoke alarms and safety matches. I love Smokey Bear.

If I cook s'mores over a campfire, I drown that fire later. I am thrilled to say that I have never actually experienced a forest fire—have you? They seem so scary. They are dangerous. And smart people know to do one thing: get out of their way!

While it might seem strange that sometimes firefighters fight fire with fire, that's what they do. Firefighters are truly brave heroes. They often save lives and homes. I sure do admire them. You might think they could not survive being overrun by a forest fire, but they often do—by covering themselves in a space blanket that protects them from the heat and flames. The surprising thing about forest fires is that while they are not so good for people and animals, they are often Mother Nature's way to clear underbrush and give a forest a fresh new start.

Well, if "where there's smoke, there's fire"...then where there's a mystery set in a forest fire, there's got to be a great read ahead of you. So grab a hose or a big glass of water and join Artemis and his family for a hot time in the old town tonight!

Carole Marsh

Christina Mimi Papa Grant

Hey, kids! As you see, here we are ready to embark on another of our exciting Carole Marsh Mystery adventures. My grandchildren often travel with me all over the world as I research new books. We have a great time together, and learn things we will carry with us for the rest of our lives!

I hope you will go to www.carolemarshmysteries.com and explore the many Carole Marsh Mysteries series!

Well, the *Mystery Girl* is all tuned up and ready for "take-off!" Gotta go...Papa says so! Wonder what I've forgotten this time?

Happy "Armchair Travel" Reading,

Mimi

About the Characters

Artemis Masters is an absentminded genius. He's a scientist at the top of his field in the early detection of natural disasters. Everyone looks to him to solve the mysteries of nature…he just needs someone to find his car keys, shoes and glasses!

Curie Masters, though only 11, has inherited her father's intelligence and ability to see things others don't. She has a natural penchant to solve mysteries…even if it means tangling with those older and supposedly smarter than her.

Nick Masters, an 8-year-old boy who's tall enough to pass as 12, likes to match wits with his sister and has her desire to solve mysteries others overlook. While he's the younger sibling, he tends to want to protect his sister, and of course, be the first to solve the mystery.

Books in this Series:

Table of Contents

CHAPTER ONE:

Hot Enough To Burn

"Can you see them yet?" Copernicus Masters asked, gawking at the fire through his high-powered binoculars. He wiped a bead of sweat off his forehead with the back of his arm. The pre-dawn temperature had already risen above 80 degrees.

The blazing yellow morning sun had just started to peek above the eastern horizon of the Yellowstone Plateau, in Yellowstone National Park, like a child's hand sneaking over the edge of a plate of cookies. To 11-year-old Curie Masters, it looked like it was hesitant to rise, as if it wasn't convinced it should make its daily appearance yet.

Curie and Copernicus, her 8-year-old brother, were hunkered down at the edge of a grassy plain. They were watching a controlled burn about four miles away. Yesterday, the fire chief explained that a controlled burn was a fire that firefighters allowed to burn to keep the forest healthy or help prevent a fire from spreading.

Copernicus, who preferred to be called "Nick," was named after Nicolaus Copernicus, the first person to propose that the sun is the center of the universe. Curie was named after Marie Curie, famous for her work on radioactivity and a two-time Nobel Prize winner. Their father, Dr. Artemis Masters, was a scientist specializing in the detection of natural disasters.

"Yeah!" Curie said, as she peered through her own set of binoculars. She glanced down at the grasslands in front of

them and spied a young deer prancing about in the tall grass. "Did you know grasslands have their own ecosystem where all living organisms work together and influence one another?" Curie asked.

"Yep," Nick replied, looking at the fire in the distance. "Last night when I was talking to Yellowstone's fire manager, Chief Thomas, he told me about the fires in 1988 that burned a lot of the park."

"In 1988?" Curie asked.

"Uh, huh," Nick said. "That year, just like this year, Yellowstone and the surrounding areas were having a severe drought, which caused **incendiary** conditions. The trees and grasses dried out and became more flammable. In fact, the summer of 1988 was the driest in Yellowstone's recorded history.

"By the end of summer," he continued, "Yellowstone had been scorched by 50 fires, not including the other 198 fires in the surrounding area. On their worst single day

of the summer, fires burned across 150,000 acres. A new fire popped up almost every day! Together, they caused a raging inferno that burned a third of the park, or over 700,000 acres, before it was over."

Nick lowered the binoculars from his eyes. "Chief Thomas said that 25,000 firefighters fought those fires during the summer! That's a lot of firemen!" he exclaimed. "Finally, in September, the first snows helped dampen the fires, and the last ones were extinguished in November."

"Did Chief Thomas say how the fires started?" Curie asked.

"No, not specifically," Nick replied. "But he did say that most fires are caused by lightning strikes. Believe it or not, there are around eight million lightning strikes across the world every day! About one percent of those strikes cause a fire. Careless people can also cause fires, like when they don't put out a campfire properly, or throw a lit cigarette out the window of their car. He said that arson is involved sometimes, too."

"Arson? I can't believe somebody would start a fire on purpose," Curie said.

"You've got to get real, big sister," Nick said. "It happens all the time. Not as much in forest fires, but there are still people who like to set fires to get insurance money or even to get revenge on people."

"That's terrible!" Curie cried. "We should do something to help people learn how to prevent forest fires."

"Hey, wait just a minute," Nick remarked with a wink, "I wouldn't want to **infringe** on Smokey Bear's territory."

CHAPTER TWO:

Maybe You Just Dreamed It

"Fire Hunters One and Two. Come in," Artemis said over the two-way radio. "This is Fire Base Central. Do you copy?"

Curie pulled the radio off a clip on her belt. "Roger, Fire Base Central," Curie said. "This is Fire Hunters One and Two. We're five by five and reading you loud and clear."

"That's great," Artemis said, "because breakfast is ready and the day is young. Hurry on back here for some crispy, tasty bacon. You copy?"

"We copy and we're on our way," Curie said. "Keep the fire hot and the orange juice cold, we'll be right back before the food grows old!"

Nick jumped to his feet, causing the young deer to bolt into the woods. "Last one there has to clean the dishes!" Nick roared, as he dashed back to their camp.

This time, Curie was prepared for Nick's antics. Whenever they went camping, he always tried to get out of doing dishes. She watched Nick as he flew through some underbrush and disappeared. Curie calmly clipped the radio to her belt and ducked into the woods, taking the shortcut back to camp that she had found yesterday when they first arrived.

Nick leaped over a log and burst into camp, his chest heaving from exertion. He skidded to a stop when he saw Curie sitting at the picnic table. She held a buttery piece of

toast in one hand and a strip of mouthwatering bacon in the other.

"No way!" Nick screamed. "How did you beat me back here? That's not possible."

"Beat you back here?" Curie questioned. "What makes you think I ever left? Maybe you just dreamed I was with you!" She smiled as she bit the bacon slice in half.

"Nick!" Artemis called. "Grab some breakfast and have a seat." Artemis was dressed in his usual oversized white lab coat. He looked like a mad scientist with a wild mop of bright red hair ringing his head. A pair of glasses balanced precariously on the end of his nose, while another pair swayed from a chain around his neck.

Nick noticed Chief Thomas sitting at the picnic table with his dad and another special visitor. He loaded his plate with cheesy scrambled eggs, sausage, and bacon and plopped down on the bench between the Chief and Smokey Bear.

Nick looked Smokey up and down. "What's up, bear?" Nick asked.

Smokey tilted his hat, which had his name written across the front, at Nick. "Hey, little buddy," Smokey said. "Remember, only you can prevent forest fires!"

"So I've been told," Nick said. "But I can't say I've ever heard it from a bear."

"Nick," Chief Thomas said, "I'd like you to meet Smokey Bear. He's going to help me later today when I talk to some schoolkids. He was interested in your father's invention, so I invited him to have breakfast with your family."

Nick shook Smokey's outstretched paw. "Good to meet you, Smokey," he said. "I've heard a lot about the work you do to make people aware of how to prevent fires."

"Well," Smokey said, "I'm happy to see that we have people like the three of you who are working to keep our firefighters healthy."

"Curie said you two were out watching the controlled burn," Chief Thomas said. "Even with those high tech glasses you were

using, you probably couldn't see any of the firefighters testing your dad's new LIPERFIRE Breathing System."

"LIPERFIRE?" Nick asked, puzzled.

"You know the government," Chief Thomas said. "We like to turn every phrase into an acronym. You call it 'LPFBS,' for Lightweight Personal Firefighting Breathing System. We decided to call it 'LIPERFIRE.' How do you like the name?"

Curie and Nick cocked their heads at each other and nodded. "It works for us!" Curie said with a grin.

"Good!" Chief Thomas exclaimed. "And LIPERFIRE is working just great so far. The men can't say enough about how light it is, how they can breathe more freely, and move around more easily when they use it." He slid his breakfast plate off to the side.

"Back to what you were saying about the fire," Nick said. "From this distance all we could see were some flames and smoke. Is that the only wildfire in the park right now?" he asked.

"No," Chief Thomas replied. "We have two small fires, which were both started a few days ago by dry lightning."

"Dry lightning?" Curie said. "Does that mean there's such a thing as wet lightning?"

"Yes, kind of," Chief Thomas answered. "When a rainy thunderstorm makes lightning, you could call it wet lightning, but a storm without rain produces dry lightning."

"Dry lightning," Smokey added, "is more common in the western part of the country because the air is much drier there than the air east of the Mississippi River."

"Exactly," Chief Thomas said. "Although in reality, a thunderstorm without rain does have rain. It's just that the rain dries up before it reaches the ground. When dry lightning reaches the dry ground, a fire is sparked but there's no rain falling to douse the flames."

"So," Nick remarked, as he scooped up another mouthful of scrambled eggs, "Smokey, since you're against fires, why do you allow controlled burns?"

"Well, Nick," Smokey explained, "natural fires can be good for a forest. Many plants and trees in a forest, like the lodgepole pine, have seeds that only open and germinate by heat. The whole ecosystem benefits when fires cause new growth and a fresh start for a forest. New growth pops up about a year after a fire. Then, the plants grow for a couple of decades, producing seeds that drop and lay dormant until another fire comes along. But, it's important that we stay in control of those fires."

"Hmm!" Nick said. "I wonder where all the animals go during a fire."

"They scatter into other areas of the forest that aren't burning," Smokey said. "Depending on when the fire occurs, some animals may be left behind because they are too young or old to travel."

"Ooohhhhh!" Curie moaned. "That's terrible."

"That's the circle of life," Nick said, "but it is a shame."

"I took a look at your father's design for the LIPERFIRE Breathing System," Smokey said, changing the subject. "It's quite **ingenious**. He said that you both helped him with it."

"A little," Curie said. "Nick came up with the particle filtration system, and I added the air moisture cooling components. But the bulk of it was Dad's idea. He's the smartest person we know!"

"Hmmm," Smokey said. "That's funny, because he says the same about you two! Smart and humble! You don't find that combination in too many humans."

Chief Thomas stood up. "Well, I've got to check on my crews, and get Smokey over to the Canyon Visitor Center. We'll see you later today, okay?"

Curie and Nick waved as they watched Smokey and Chief Thomas drive away. "As bears go," Nick said, "that Smokey is a pretty nice guy."

"You're a piece of work," Curie said, grinning at her brother.

Neither of them saw the column of smoke just beginning to rise in the distance.

CHAPTER THREE:

Hey, Dude! What About The Fire?

Tom shoved his arms through the straps of his backpack and hoisted it onto his shoulders. He kicked Ralph's feet. Ralph was sprawled on a bedroll next to last night's campfire.

"Hey, dude," Tom said. "Are you ready to go?"

Ralph sat up and stretched. "Dude, the sun's not even up yet," he mumbled.

"No kidding!" Tom replied, munching on a granola bar. "It'll be up in a few minutes. We've got a lot of ground to cover and I want to hitch a ride as soon as we can. According to our list of things to see," Tom said, tapping the paper in his hand, "Mammoth Hot Springs is next on the list and that's only a few miles up the road. Then we need to cut back and head down to the Canyon Visitor Center this afternoon. We'll find a place to camp for the night down there."

"Okay, okay," Ralph groaned. As he slowly rose to his feet, his fingers rubbed the medallion on the thick gold chain around his neck.

"Come on, Ralph," Tom said. "This trip is supposed to brighten you up, man. You said you wanted to get away. You've got to put her out of your mind. It's over, and it's time for you to move on."

"I'm trying, man," Ralph said, still holding onto the medallion. "Let me roll this up and I'll be ready to go."

Ralph tied the bedroll to his backpack and whipped it onto his shoulders. As he did,

one of the flaps on the bulging pockets popped open. A plastic bag flew out and landed under the corner of a small boulder. Ralph jammed his favorite baseball cap on his head and began to follow Tom out of their campsite. A gust of wind blew Ralph's cap off his head. He stumbled back to get it and noticed a wisp of smoke curling from the fire pit they had built the night before.

"Hey, dude!" Ralph shouted. "What about the fire?"

"Dude!" Tom yelled. "Don't worry, I checked it. It's out. Come on, man, we've got to get moving."

"Okay!" Ralph shouted, jogging to catch up to his buddy.

The two campers hiked out of the dense foliage to Grand Loop Road and spotted a van heading toward Mammoth. They both stuck out their thumbs to hitch a ride. The van slowed to a stop, and they scrambled inside just as another strong breeze whipped across the road.

Seconds later, the same breeze blew through the trees, around fallen logs, past dense bushes, and over the top of Tom and Ralph's campfire, easily blowing the top layer of ash from the burnt branches and twigs. Small coals glowed to life as fresh oxygen fed the embers of the not-so-dead campfire. Another breeze picked up several of the glowing embers and whisked them into a pile of dried grass. Soon, smoke began to rise and, as if by magic, small flames flickered. The tiny fire grew with each gust of wind, swallowing more grass and sucking in more oxygen.

The already warm day was about to get much hotter.

CHAPTER FOUR:

This Fire's Not Going Away Quickly

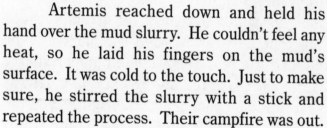

Artemis reached down and held his hand over the mud slurry. He couldn't feel any heat, so he laid his fingers on the mud's surface. It was cold to the touch. Just to make sure, he stirred the slurry with a stick and repeated the process. Their campfire was out.

About twenty minutes earlier, Nick had poured two buckets of water over the morning fire. Curie took a small shovel and dug up some dirt, which she piled on top of the wet coals. They both used sticks to stir the combination of coals, water, and dirt into mud, and then let it sit while they packed up the rest of their campsite.

That fire extinguishing exercise had become their routine when camping. Nick and Curie would put out the fire in the proper manner, and Artemis would check it about twenty minutes later just before they left camp.

Curie and Nick were already settled in the van, which they proudly called the MOD— for Masters of Disaster. As Artemis loaded the tent into the storage compartment, he noticed the new Yellowstone bumper sticker Curie had plastered on the back door. It was surrounded by a mass of brightly colored stickers from all the other places the family had visited. A slew of antennae stuck out at odd angles from the van's roof, giving it a quirky, extraterrestrial look.

Artemis slid into the driver's seat, whacking his forehead on the sun visor. "Ouch," he mumbled. "I always forget about

that thing." He rubbed the bump growing under his curly red hair. "Are we ready?" he asked.

"Check! We're loaded and ready to roll," Nick said, strapping his skinny frame into the passenger seat, or as they referred to it, the "Command-Com" seat next to his father. It was his turn to be co-pilot.

"Have our LIPERFIRE systems been double-checked?" Artemis asked.

"Yes, sir!" shouted Curie from the rear of the van. "They're prepped and ready for use."

"Great," Artemis said. "Pilot to co-pilot. All systems go?"

"Roger that, Captain," Nick said in a deep voice, sliding his sunglasses over his eyes. "All systems are A-OK. Kick the tires and light the fires!"

Artemis was about to give Nick the thumbs up when he realized that he had forgotten a small detail—to start the engine! He reached for the keys in the ignition, but they weren't there. Something about this seemed awfully familiar, like it had happened before. He was about to search his pockets when Nick dangled the keys in front of his face.

"Dad," Nick said, "don't you remember? You always leave them in the cup holder."

"Oh, yeah!" Artemis said. "You know, if I remembered everything, I wouldn't need a co-pilot, would I?"

"Point taken," Nick replied. "So, let's kick those tires and light the fires. We've got work to do!"

Artemis cranked the engine to life, flipped down the clip-on sunglasses over his prescription eyeglasses, and threw the van into gear.

Nick adjusted the multi-band radio in the van to pick up the fire department frequency Chief Thomas gave them. He loved to listen to fire or police bands when they drove because he found it interesting and because it irritated his sister. Most of the department chatter today was about the controlled burns the firefighters were monitoring.

"Chief," called a voice on the radio. "Fire One here. We just got notification of a wildfire in sector four. I've rolled crews three, four, and five."

"Why three crews?" Chief Thomas replied. Nick already knew why, and he knew the chief did, too.

"It's a big one, Chief," Fire One said. "And it's getting bigger. As you know, sector four is the driest part of the park. I've got evacuation teams out and I've called for backup crews." The voice on the radio crackled. "This one's not going away quickly."

CHAPTER FIVE:

Longitude And Latitude

"Okay," Chief Thomas said. "Have crews one and two put out the controlled burns. We're going to need them in sector four ASAP. Give me the coordinates."

"Roger that!" Fire One said. "We're staging off North Grand Loop Road at 44 degrees, 57 minutes, and 10 seconds north and 110 degrees, 36 minutes, and 34 seconds west." Nick rapidly punched the numbers into the Global Positioning System (GPS) unit mounted on the dashboard. He pictured Chief Thomas doing the same thing.

"Artemis," Chief Thomas said, "I'm pretty sure you're listening in. Since we're putting out the two controlled burns, meet me at the coordinates given. I want you there in case we have any problems with the LIPERFIRE systems."

Artemis nodded his head. He knew Chief Thomas was concerned about his firefighters.

"Fire One," Chief Thomas said, "you know the drill. Get some firebreaks built, widen the existing ones, and get the water bombers up. Have them start dropping some fire retardant. Also, call Evergreen Aviation and see if we can put their two supertankers on standby, loaded and ready to drop."

"Roger," Fire One said. "We're on it, but forecasts show the winds picking up. I'm not sure how effective they'll be."

"Roger," Chief Thomas said. "Throw as many resources at it as possible. I don't want this to turn into another 1988. One fire like that in a lifetime is enough. I'll be there in twenty. Keep me informed."

Artemis followed the GPS directions displayed on the glowing screen. It would take some time to get there. "Quiz time, kids," he said. "Curie, what did those coordinates mean?"

"That's easy," Curie said. "The two sets of numbers are for longitude and latitude. They give us a way to locate certain points on the earth."

Curie remembered an example her favorite science teacher had used in school. "If you take a ball," she said, "and draw equally spaced vertical lines from top to bottom, that's longitude, which measures distance from east to west. If you draw a horizontal line around the center of the ball, that's the earth's equator. If you draw equally spaced horizontal lines around the ball going up and down from the equator, you will be drawing latitude lines. Latitude measures distance from north to south. Both latitude and longitude can be divided into smaller measurements called minutes and seconds to pinpoint a location precisely."

"Very good," Artemis said. "Now here's one for you, Nick. This is a two-part question. First, why is fire retardant red? Second, after fire retardant is dropped on the flames, how long does it take to put the fire out?"

"Man," Nick said. "For a minute there, I thought you were going to give me something hard. Fire retardant, or foscheck, is a mixture of water and a red, powdered fire retardant. It's red because it creates a contrast with the green foliage, which helps the pilots see where they've already dropped the retardant."

Nick turned in his seat to face his dad. "And your second question is a trick question," he said. "Contrary to what many people may think, water bombing, or dropping water or fire retardant, doesn't put out a fire. It just creates another firebreak, or an area where the fire can't get through easily. It helps

prevent trees and other foliage on the edge of the fire from catching fire, too."

Nick glanced at the GPS to make sure they were still on track. "Firefighters can't help the trees that are already burning," he continued. "Plus, pilots won't drop directly onto a fire, because the heat from the fire would **evaporate** the water, or the retardant, before it had a chance to work. So, the idea behind dropping is to contain the fire where it's at, to allow the fire to run out of fuel, and to put out any fire on the edge, where it's just starting."

"I thought I had you with that question," Artemis said with a smile. "How was I ever blessed with not just one, but two incredibly intelligent children?"

Artemis continued his quiz until they got closer to the staging area. As the MOD van careened around a bend in the road, Curie and Nick saw a layer of smoke over the forest ahead. Artemis whipped the van into the staging area, spraying rocks into the air.

CHAPTER SIX:

Smokejumping

Chief Thomas was trying to calm a frantic man standing next to one of the fire trucks. "You can't just leave them in there!" the man cried, waving his arms as he talked. "They'll die! I've got thousands of dollars invested in those two horses. They're thoroughbreds, and if I lose them I'm finished!"

"I'm sorry," Chief Thomas said. "I can't allow anyone but professional firefighters to go in there. This fire is growing fast and we don't have enough firelines set up to even think about getting it under control any time soon."

"But, but..." the man said.

"I'm sorry, sir," Chief Thomas said. "All I can do is let the firefighters know to keep their eyes open for them." The chief turned and marched toward Artemis and the kids.

A firefighter grabbed his arm. "Chief," he said, "the smokejumpers got in safely, but they say it's spreading too fast so they're retreating to the south."

"Okay," Chief Thomas said. "Are we ready for the briefing?"

"All comm links will be up in five minutes," the firefighter replied. "The men are ready."

"Good," Chief Thomas said. "I'll be there in a minute." He turned back toward Artemis and shook his hand. "Welcome to the party!"

"Chief, we hope we can help in some way," Artemis said. "What's happening?"

"Well," the Chief said, "you heard about the smokejumpers..."

Curie and Nick were standing next to their dad. "What's a smokejumper?" Curie asked.

"They're just about the bravest men in the world," Nick said. "Their job is to get a jump on the fire to keep it from spreading. They parachute into the center of a fire shortly after it starts. Can you imagine that? They jump out of a perfectly good airplane just so they can fall through a bunch of burning trees in the middle of a fire."

"Wow!" Curie said. "They sound like real heroes."

"That's for sure!" Nick said. "I think it takes a special type of person to be that brave."

"You're right," Chief Thomas said. "It does. But this time, because of the dry conditions and the wind, this fire is spreading too fast for them to handle it. It's been less than two hours and it's already burned around 800 acres."

"Did that man you were talking with lose a couple of horses?" Artemis asked.

"Yes," Chief Thomas said. "He's traveling to a race and stopped in the park for the night. He decided to take the horses out of their trailer, which was a really bad idea. The fire spooked them and they took off."

"Wouldn't they run away from the fire?" Nick asked.

"Normally, yes," the chief said. "But the wind changed directions about an hour ago and the fire has them trapped up in the highlands over there." Chief Thomas pointed toward a hilly area a few miles downwind of them.

The chief scanned the children's faces. "I hear you two want to get close to a fire. Is that true?"

"It sure is, sir!" Nick said. "We're ready to report for duty."

"Great," the chief said. "Grab your LIPERFIRE breathing systems and meet me at the briefing tent. I'll take you out to where we think the fire may have started. From what I hear, they've got that area under control." He shook Artemis' hand again. "Are you sure you don't want to join us?"

"I'm sure," Artemis said.

"Okay," Chief Thomas said. "I'll get these two back to you safely."

"Thanks," Artemis said. "And good luck. I hope you know that everyone realizes you guys are true heroes. It's easy to run from a fire, but it takes a brave person, like Nick said, or maybe a little bit crazy person, to run into a fire. We all know that your men are among the bravest in the world."

CHAPTER SEVEN:

You've Got 30 Minutes!

Artemis fidgeted in the MOD van. "Come on, John!" he snapped into his cell phone. Artemis had met John in college. A few years after graduating, he helped John get an engineering job with NASA. "You owe me! You wouldn't have that great job with NASA if I hadn't..."

"All right, all right!" John said. "I can get you 30 minutes maximum. Give me your information and I'll transfer control of the satellite to you in 60 seconds, okay?"

"Okay," Artemis said. He gave John his computer access information.

"What do you need this for, anyway?" John asked.

"Horses," Artemis said. "I need to find a couple of lost horses."

"Forget I even asked," John said. "It's yours in 5, 4, 3, 2, 1."

Suddenly, Artemis' computer desktop image disappeared. A NASA control screen replaced it. "Thanks, John," he said. "I appreciate your help."

"You've got 30 minutes so just get it done," John said. "I'll be taking back control at exactly that time."

Artemis pounded away at the keyboard, and then adjusted one of the knobs on the console in front of him. One of the antennae

on the roof of the van rotated to face the satellite 22 miles above it.

What Artemis was about to do was probably like trying to find a needle in a haystack, but he had to try. He wasn't doing it for the careless owner, but because Artemis loved horses. He grew up on a farm and until the day he'd gone off to college, he rode his horse, Charlie, every day.

Artemis calculated the probable path the horses would have taken based on the terrain, wind direction, and pure guesswork. His method was not completely scientific, but sometimes you just had to go with a hunch.

Minutes ticked by quickly, as image after image sailed across his monitor. Artemis was watching thermal images that showed differences in temperature. He could spot a cool boulder in the middle of the raging fire.

He figured the horses would try to keep ahead of the smoke, so he zoomed in on an area where the horses would probably end up. Twenty-eight minutes had passed already.

If he didn't find them in the next two minutes, it wouldn't matter. He spun another dial and the image grew even larger.

Two cooler images suddenly appeared at the base of a small gulley. There they were!

He had 60 seconds left. Artemis yanked his high-tech cell phone off his belt and plugged it into the computer.

Thirty seconds left. He typed furiously.

Twenty seconds. The computer began to download the coordinates into the phone's GPS software.

Ten seconds. Images of the terrain appeared.

Five seconds. The best path to the coordinates came into view.

His computer went blank.

Oh, no, Artemis thought. Have I lost everything? Suddenly, a popup window appeared. It read:

CHAPTER EIGHT:

RATTLE! RATTLE!

The LIPERFIRE system on Artemis' back was performing beautifully. He pulled hard on the strap that wrapped around his ribcage as he dutifully followed the GPS map he'd downloaded onto his cell phone. He was within three feet of the map's coordinates.

Smoke swirled around him with every breeze that passed through the trees. So far he hadn't encountered the main fire. If the wind didn't change, he and the horses should be safe. To make sure the horses would follow him, he'd grabbed a handful of sugar cubes at the food tent near the staging area.

Artemis came to a small creek about ten feet wide. I'm not going in there, Artemis thought. I *hate* getting my feet wet. He walked a few yards upstream and found a fallen tree lying across the creek. That's the ticket, he thought, and promptly jumped on the log to cross the creek. He glanced at the cell phone in his hand and froze.

A shiny rattlesnake slithered onto the opposite end of the downed tree. Its tongue darted in and out of its mouth. Artemis started to tiptoe off the tree and slipped just as the snake sprang at him. His cell phone flew out of his hands.

CHAPTER NINE:

Fire Tornadoes

Chief Thomas brought Nick and Curie to an area of the forest where the fire had burned out and moved on. Curie watched the chief talk to one of his firefighters, straining to hear what they were saying.

Nick circled what looked like the remains of a rocked-in campfire pit. The rocks were scorched black on one side of the pit. I'll bet that's the direction the wind was blowing, Nick thought. As he looked up to tell Curie, his eye caught something on the ground at the base of a nearby boulder. It was a plastic bag. He scooped it up and dropped it in his pocket without looking inside.

Chief Thomas hurried over to the kids. "I just got confirmation that this was where the fire started," he said. "It looks like someone didn't put out their campfire properly and the wind took care of the rest."

"There's no way to tell whose campfire it was, is there?" Curie asked.

"Nope," Chief Thomas said. "We don't register campers outside of the formal camping areas. Are you guys ready to get a little closer to the fire?"

"Yessss!" Nick blurted. "The closer, the better!"

Chief Thomas waved down a truck heading toward one of the firelines and they all climbed aboard. As they approached the line, Nick couldn't believe the intense activity. Firefighters were everywhere, clearing brush, spraying fire retardant, and bulldozing a firebreak all the way down to bare earth.

"Let's get a move on!" one of the firefighters cried. "We've got one hour!"

Other crews manned water tankers, soaking vegetation to keep it from igniting.

Firefighters were doused by water from the tankers.

OWWWOOOOOO!

A howling sound accompanied the approaching fire. "What is that?" Nick cried, grabbing Curie's arm. A fiery funnel that looked like a tornado appeared before them. The flames swirling about it shot 100 feet into the sky.

"That's a fire tornado," Chief Thomas shouted. "When two different air masses run into each other, the result is an upward air current that carries the surrounding flames. It forms a whirl, or a tornado-like funnel effect. It looks cool, but fire tornadoes can make fires even more dangerous!"

Chief Thomas wiped the sweat off his forehead with a dingy white handerchief. "In 1923, near Tokyo, Japan," he continued, "an earthquake ignited a city-wide fire, resulting

in a gigantic fire tornado that killed 38,000 people in just 15 minutes! In 1926, a four-day fire led to thousands of fire tornadoes in California."

"I've read about fire tornadoes," Nick said. "Aren't most of them spawned by wildfires?"

"Yes," said Chief Thomas. "Fire tornadoes can range in height from 30 to 200 feet, but they're usually only 10 feet wide. Most of them only last a few minutes. But I've got firefighters here who have seen big ones last for more than 20 minutes."

A firefighter covered with black soot raced up to Chief Thomas. "Chief," the firefighter said, "I think it's time to get these youngsters out of the way. The fire will be at the break in just a few minutes."

"Okay, guys," Chief Thomas said. "It's time for us to get back to the staging area. You can monitor the fire from there with me."

"That sounds great," Curie said.

"Yeah," Nick added, "but first we need to check on our dad."

As he climbed into the truck, Nick felt the plastic bag in his pocket and wondered what secrets it might hold.

CHAPTER TEN:

Where's Dad?

Curie and Nick scurried to the van after returning from the fireline. Nick noticed Chief Thomas rush into the control tent with several other firefighters.

Curie scanned the inside of the van for her dad. He wasn't there and he wasn't near any of the tents, either. "Where could Dad be?" she asked.

"I don't know," Nick replied. "Let's call him."

"That's a good idea," Curie said, digging in her desk drawer for her cell phone. Artemis didn't want them to carry cell phones everywhere they went, like most kids. But he let Curie have one to keep in the van in case she needed to make a call.

"Hey, everyone. This is Artemis, and if you're hearing this recording it means I'm not able to talk at the moment. Try calling back again, and let's have a nice long chat."

"Did he answer?" Nick asked.

"No," Curie replied. She dialed her dad's phone over and over. No answer. *Where could he be? Why didn't he answer?*

CHAPTER ELEVEN:

It Takes A Crazy Person

The snake lunged at Artemis, just missing him as he tumbled off the log into the creek. Miraculously, he caught his cell phone in mid air, but stuck his hand in the water to push him to his feet. He scrambled across the creek through knee-deep water. The rattler lost interest and slid away to escape the smoke.

Once back on shore, Artemis tried the phone to see if it still worked. It squeaked a few times, and then shut itself down.

"That's not good," he said. He took the back cover off and removed the battery. "So much for technology." Artemis blew as much water as he could out of the phone, dried off the battery, and put the phone back together. Hopefully, it would dry out quickly and he could try it again.

Artemis went back to the riverbank and looked up into the low mountains. He closed his eyes and visualized the map image on the phone. When his eyes popped open, he smiled and started to climb up the mountainside.

The smoke was getting thicker and the visibility in front of him was decreasing. Luckily, he hadn't hurt his waterproof LIPERFIRE system. It was still functioning normally. Without it, he would be in big trouble. A voice in the back of his mind started to question the wisdom of going off into a fire all by himself. Then something he'd said to Chief Thomas popped into his head.

"It's easy to run from a fire, but it takes a brave man or a maybe a little bit crazy person to run into a fire." He suddenly realized that he must be a bit crazy, because he certainly wasn't that brave.

CHAPTER TWELVE:

Listen And Learn, Little Brother!

"Where could he be?" Curie asked, her voice trembling.

"Don't worry," Nick said. "Knowing Dad, he's probably got a firefighter cornered, while he tells him how the LIPERFIRE system works."

"Yeah," Curie said. "You're probably right."

"Check this out," Nick said, as he removed the plastic bag from his pocket and dumped the contents onto his lap. "I found it at the site where the fire started."

"Are you crazy?" Curie shouted. "That's evidence in a fire investigation. It could be used to **implicate** the person at that campfire. Nick, you can get in a lot of trouble for taking that."

"Not if it helps us find the careless people who started the fire," Nick said. "Let's see. We have a used train ticket stub from Chicago, Illinois to Billings, Montana, a piece of notebook paper with a list of places to see, a pack of chewing gum, and a gold chain with a gold apostrophe charm or something hanging on it. I'll bet you the person is a writer. Who else would wear an apostrophe around their neck?"

"Nick," Curie said.   "That's not an apostrophe."

"It's not?" Nick asked.

"No!" Curie said with a giggle. "It's half of a Yin Yang medallion necklace."

"Oh?" Nick said. "So, where is the other half and is this piece the Yin or the Yang? I mean, can anyone tell the Yin from the Yang? They're like identical twins."

"You know," Curie said, "if I were a duck, I'd be quacking up right now. I think the answer to your question will help us find the person at that campfire last night."

"Okay, Daffy Duck," Nick said, examining the other objects from the bag. "The gum tells us that this person was trying to stop smoking."

"Why do you think that?" Curie said. "Everyone chews gum."

"Yeah," Nick said, showing Curie the pack of gum, "but only people who want to quit smoking chew this kind of gum. The train ticket only tells where the person came from and not where they are going."

"That's true," Curie said, picking up the piece of notebook paper. "But what does this list tell us?" Curie scanned the list. "The first stop after Billings is Tower Junction."

"That's not too far from here," Nick said. "Maybe we should go and check it out."

"We don't have the time to check out all the places on the list," Curie said. "We have to use deductive reasoning to figure out where the person is now. Does the train ticket have any dates or times on it?"

"Yeah," Nick said, looking over the ticket. "It's for the day before yesterday. The person arrived in Billings about 8 p.m."

"Perfect," Curie said. "That means they most likely didn't leave Billings until the next day, which means it probably took them most of the day to hitch a ride to Tower Junction. There's not much to do there, so they probably only stayed a little while, and then headed toward the next place on their list."

"Whoa, Nelly," Nick said. "You keep saying they and them, and instead of hitching a ride, they could have their own car."

"Listen and learn, little brother!" Curie said. "I overheard a firefighter talking to the chief. He found two sets of footprints at the campsite and the same two sets of prints out by the road. There was no way to park a vehicle of any size other than a motorcycle, and the firefighter said there were no

motorcycle tracks. So, they had to be traveling on foot hitching rides."

"Free spirits, huh," Nick said.

"Or someone who didn't have a lot of money to travel or stay at a motel," Curie said.

"Okay," Nick said. "So, if they camped there last night, where would they be heading today?"

"According to this list, Mammoth Springs," Curie said, "which isn't too far from where they were camping." Curie looked at her wristwatch. "But I don't think they're there."

"Why not?" Nick asked.

"See these little dashes after Billings and Tower Junction?" Curie said.

Nick looked at the list. "Yeah," he said. "What do you think they are?"

"I think they indicate what they plan on seeing in a day, because there's no mark after Mammoth, but there is one after their next stop, the Canyon Visitor Center. I think that's where they'll be this afternoon."

"Cool," Nick said. "Now we just need to find a way to get down there."

"And leave a note for Dad," Curie said, as she scribbled a quick note, "so he knows where we are." She perched the note on the desk next to another folded piece of paper with their names on the outside. Unfortunately, Curie didn't notice it. The note inside read,

Curie and Nick,

    I'm off on a mission of utmost importance. I know where the horses are, and in good conscience I couldn't leave them to die without at least trying to get them to safety. You know how much I love horses. Let's keep this between the three of us. If you need me just call my cell.

                Love,
                Dad

CHAPTER THIRTEEN:

Sugar Cubes

Artemis studied the compass built into his watch. He was sure he was heading in the right direction. He'd been hiking uphill for close to an hour and was getting thirsty and tired. He sat on a small boulder and took a drink of water from the canteen he carried on his hip. He pulled an energy bar out of his pocket and quickly gobbled it down.

In less than a minute, he was moving again. "Finding the horses is going to be the easy part," he said to himself. "Getting them out of here through all this smoke will be the hard part." He figured he had to be very close

to the horses.   Artemis scanned the
ground in front of him. He didn't want to run
into any more fleeing snakes, let alone some
other scared animal. The visibility had
improved slightly, which meant that the fire
wasn't advancing in his direction too quickly.

*WEEEHEEEHEEE!
WEEEHEEEHEEE!*

The horses! He followed the sounds
into a gulley and through some underbrush.

*WEEEHEEEHEEE!
WEEEHEEEHEEE!*

The whinnies were growing louder,
but also more frantic. When he popped out
of the brush, there they were! They
reared up on their back legs in fear. "Whoa,
boys," Artemis said softly. "It's okay, I'm here
to help. Come on, everything's going to
be okay."

The horses did not respond to Artemis' plea. They backed away and continued to whinny. Artemis realized what was wrong. He quickly snapped off his LIPERFIRE face mask.

"Okay, boys," Artemis tried again. "It's okay, I'm here to help." He moved slowly toward them. "Come on. Everything is going to be okay." He pulled a couple of sugar cubes out of his backpack and held them out in front of him as he slowly stepped toward the horses. They stopped moving and quieted down. Artemis couldn't believe how beautiful they were.

Each horse took a cube from his outstretched hand. As they munched on the treat, he stroked their necks. "You guys are going to be okay. We'll find our way out of the fire, don't you worry," he said softly.

Artemis slowly took their reins and offered two more sugar cubes to the horses. "Okay," he said. "Let's get moving." He gently pulled on the reins and the horses obediently followed him.

Artemis took two steps and stopped. Above the treetops in front of him, the sky glowed a bright orange. A stiff breeze blew smoke into his face, and he quickly put his facemask back on. The wind had shifted.

CHAPTER FOURTEEN:

Wish In One Hand, Spit In The Other

Curie and Nick were sitting in the back seat of a pickup. They'd told Chief Thomas they wanted to see Smokey Bear again at the Canyon Visitor Center. He found them a ride, and now they were only a few minutes from their destination.

"I wish Dad was with us," Curie said.

"You know what Grandma always says," Nick said. "Wish in one hand, spit in the other. You get the same thing—nothing!"

Curie laughed. "Yeah," she said. "She's right about that."

"How are we going to be able to find the person we're looking for?" Nick asked.

"I think we need to come up with a profile of what the person would look like," Curie said. "Odds are that it's a man."

"Why?" Nick asked.

"Because," Curie said, "there are only a handful of women who are willing to sleep out under the stars with all those bugs crawling around. Guys love it."

"Good point!" Nick said. "Okay, so we've got an adult male wearing a gold Yin or Yang medallion. I think we should also be looking for this guy to be with another person. Using your thoughts on women campers, it would probably be another guy."

"I agree," Curie said.

"Also," Nick added, "the train ticket makes me believe that the person is from Chicago. From what Dad has told me, Chicagoans love sports. Maybe, just maybe, the person will be wearing something with a

Chicago team's name on it like the Cubs, Bears, White Sox, or even the Black Hawks."

"That's possible," Curie said, "but the main thing to look for is the medallion."

"True," Nick said. "But if we are to consider the whole profile, we're looking for two males. One of them may be wearing a medallion, a Chicago sports team item, and quite possibly be chewing gum.

"That's so funny," Curie said.

"What's funny?" Nick asked.

"That you're so much like Dad," Curie said. "Minus the forgetfulness, of course. He always wants to consider even the remotest information."

"Thanks for the compliment," Nick said.

"You're welcome," Curie said. "I'm still worried about him not calling us back yet, but knowing him, he's probably having the time of his life!"

CHAPTER FIFTEEN:

Red Showers

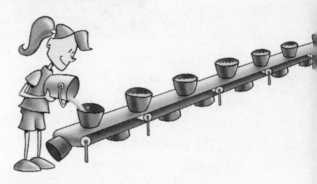

Artemis was sitting on top of Zig. For fun, he'd named the horses Zig and Zag. The two horses could pass for twins except Zig had a long streak of white down the front of his nose.

"Okay, boy," Artemis said, pressing his heels lightly into Zig's sides. They needed to get out of here—quick! The fire was so close! Now he could see it through the trees.

WHOOP! WHOOP!

The Fire Service helicopter passed directly overhead. The horses whinnied and began to step back and forth anxiously. Artemis pulled on the reins. "Whoa, boy," he said. He yanked his backpack off his shoulders and unzipped a pocket on the front. He whipped out a poncho and quickly unfolded it. He pulled on Zag's reins to bring his head close to Zig's. Then, he laid the poncho over their heads and bent over so his face was pointing to the ground.

The red rain of watery fire retardant lasted less than a minute. As soon as it ended, he slid the poncho from their eyes and tucked it back into the backpack.

"Giddy up, boy," Artemis said. A few minutes later, he had to stop and repeat the process with the poncho, as another

helicopter approached. After the red rain,
Artemis yanked the poncho off the horses
again, but this time he held onto it, figuring
he'd need it again.

"Giddy up, boy," Artemis urged. He
tried not to look at how close the fire was,
but focus on trying to keep up a steady pace.
It had been warm all day, but as the fire grew
closer, he was starting to feel like someone
had stuck him in a roasting pot. Without
the LIPERFIRE breathing system, he would
not have been able to keep going. He
didn't know how much longer the horses
would last.

CRACK!
BAM!

A burning tree crashed across his path.
The impact startled Zig, and he reared back

on his hind legs. Artemis wrapped his arms around Zig's neck. "It's okay, boy," he said softly into Zig's ear. Zig calmed down.

"We're blocked," Artemis said to the horses, as if they were listening. Artemis turned Zig and Zag into a thicket of bushes. As soon as they reached the other side, he spotted a deer trail. Let's take it, he thought.

Zig seemed determined to continue forward. Artemis decided to let the horse use his instincts. It was a good decision—Zig led Artemis and Zag to a bubbling creek, where all three gulped the fresh water.

Artemis decided to follow the path of the creek. His eyes widened as he saw tree after tree burst into flames behind him. He urged Zig to trot faster, pulling a fearful Zag behind them. Although they were moving at a good clip, the fire was gaining on them, crackling like a raging monster in the trees around them. Gone were the normal peaceful sounds of the forest. All Artemis could hear

were trees snapping, crackling, and popping, or CRASHING to the ground or into other trees.

Zig came to a sudden halt. What's the matter? Artemis thought. He walked the horses forward a few steps and realized they were standing on the edge of a cliff looming 20 feet above the ground below.

Without saying a word, Artemis looked behind him. The forest was ablaze!

CHAPTER SIXTEEN:

Too Smart For Their Own Good

Chief Thomas knocked on the door to the MOD van. He had to tell Artemis they were moving the staging area back down the road a few miles. After the wind shift, the fire had started moving in their direction. He knocked again. When no one answered, he opened the door and stepped inside.

"Artemis!" he shouted. No answer. Chief Thomas moved past the desks to the back to see if anyone was in the back of the van. No one was there. As he turned to leave, he saw the note Artemis had left for the kids.

He picked it up, read it, and shook his head. "Artemis!" he cried. "Why did you go after those horses?"

He snatched the other piece of paper on the desk. It read,

Dad,

We're off on a mission of utmost importance. We think we know where to find the person who caused the fire. We didn't want to tell Chief Thomas until we were sure. Call us when you get this message. Let's keep this between the three of us.

Love,
Curie and Nick

"Oh, that's just great!" Chief Thomas said, leaping out of the van. "Those children are just as bad as their father. They all may be too smart for their own good!"

CHAPTER SEVENTEEN:

GERONIMO!

"We don't have much much of a choice," Artemis said to the horses, as he looked down toward the lake shoreline at the bottom of the cliff. "The shore isn't too far. We should be able to swim to it, boys." He patted Zig's neck.

Artemis backed the horses up about 30 feet from the edge of the cliff. He pulled his cell phone from his pocket and sealed it in a plastic bag he had tucked in his backpack. He stuffed the plastic bag back in his pocket. He yanked the LIPERFIRE system and backpack from his shoulders.

"GERONIMO!"

Artemis shouted, as he slapped Zig sharply on his rump.

Zig and Zag shot forward, reaching the cliff's edge at the same time.

The two thoroughbreds leaped into the air over the lake.

CHAPTER EIGHTEEN:

Little Red Ridinghood

Nick and Curie strolled through the Canyon Visitor Center looking for anyone meeting the profile they'd created. "We're probably wasting our time," Nick said. "We've been looking around here for almost an hour."

"Patience, little brother, patience," Curie said. She pulled the hood of her red jacket over her head. "It's cold in here. I think they'll show up before it gets dark."

"Why do you think that?" Nick asked.

"Would you like to be out on a dark road in the middle of a forest with all those wild animals, like bears and wolves?" Curie said. "I know I wouldn't."

"I don't know, Little Red Ridinghood," Nick said. "I think you just have a problem with forests—and maybe wolves."

"Thanks," Curie said, seeing her reflection in a nearby window. "Don't you know it's not polite to tease a girl? What if I had a sensitive personality? You could be leaving an emotional scar on my psyche that may never heal. I could grow up feeling inferior because of a comment like that."

Curie tried to contain her laughter, but the last few words came out with a giggle.

"Yeah," Nick said. "You're sensitive all right. About as sensitive as a..."

A deep voice boomed behind them. "Remember, children. Only you can prevent forest fires!"

Nick whirled around. "Smokey Bear!" Nick said. "How are you? Long time no see."

"I'm doing very well, Nick," Smokey said. "I just finished my last tour group. What are you two doing here? I thought you were going to be with Chief Thomas today."

Nick wasn't fully listening to Smokey, because he was watching Curie. She was staring at a group of people who had just entered the center. "We were with him earlier," Nick said. "He, uh..."

"Come on, Nick," Curie said, pulling him away from Smokey Bear. "Sorry, Smokey, we have some business to take care of."

Smokey Bear nodded his massive brown head.

"Do you see them?" Curie whispered.

Nick looked past the crowd. Two young men in their mid-twenties were standing by a display. One of them wore a Chicago Cubs baseball cap and a gold chain around his tanned neck. Nick couldn't see a medallion though, because the bottom of the chain was in his shirt. The funny thing was—the guy was chewing gum.

"Come on," Curie yanked him again, dragging her brother across the floor toward the two men.

"Excuse me," Curie said. "I love that chain you're wearing. Where did you get it?"

"This?" Ralph said, pulling the chain out from under his shirt. "It was something I bought for my fiancée when we first met."

"So," Curie said. "You probably want the other half of it, then." She pulled out the bag and handed the medallion piece to Ralph.

Ralph opened the bag. "Whoa," he said. "Where did you find this?"

"Nick," Curie said, pointing to her brother, "found it by the campfire you guys had last night off Grand Loop Road."

"You were by our campfire?" Tom asked. "Why?"

"We were with the fire chief," Curie said. She turned and saw Smokey Bear, with his arms crossed over his chest, watching the group intently. Chief Thomas quickly marched toward them.

"You two have a lot of explaining to do," Chief Thomas said to Nick and Curie. "You—"

"Chief Thomas," Nick interrupted, "I'd like you to meet the two gentlemen who didn't put out their fire the proper way this morning, and caused the fire your men are now fighting."

"What are you talking about, kid?" Tom cried.

"Dude, you said you put the fire out!" Ralph shouted.

"I...I thought I did!" Tom said. "What proof does this kid have? How do you know it was our fire? Oh, man!"

CHAPTER NINETEEN:

Chips Off The Old Block

Chief Thomas pulled the truck up close to the shoreline. An ambulance was right behind him, followed by the owner of the horses in a massive horse trailer. Nick and Curie jumped out of the truck to check on their father. Artemis shivered under a scratchy burlap blanket.

"What was it you told me about being brave or crazy?" Chief Thomas asked. "It may be brave to run into a fire, but it sure is crazy to jump off a cliff."

"Yeah!" Artemis said wearily. "You are absolutely right!"

The owner of Zig and Zag ran up to his horses. "Oh, my boys!" he cried. He ran his hands over them to see if they were okay, and slowly led them to their trailer. He stopped by the emergency vehicle where the paramedics were checking Artemis. "Thank you for saving them," he said to Artemis. "How can I ever repay you?"

"You're welcome," Artemis said. "These are some pretty brave horses. You should be proud." Zig nuzzled Artemis' hand, and he patted the side of the horse's neck. "Good boy," he said. Artemis looked up at the owner. "There's no need to repay me. Seeing these horses alive is good enough for me."

After the horses were gone, Artemis turned to Chief Thomas. "How bad is the fire?"

"Not as bad as it could have been," the chief said. "With the help of the supertankers

we've got 60 percent of it under control."
Chief Thomas pointed to the darkening sky.
"And with the help of Mother Nature, we may
be able to contain the rest."

"He's healthy as an ox, Chief," the
emergency technician said, "and no worse the
wear from his exploit."

"Good," the chief said. "Just so you
know, your LIPERFIRE breathing systems
exceeded our expectations! We'll need a lot
more of them. Between you guys and the
supertankers, the face of fighting a forest fire
is changing."

"Great!" Artemis said. "We'll get right
on it!"

"And by the way," Chief Thomas said,
"both you, and these two," he pointed to Nick
and Curie, "exceeded my expectations, too."

Artemis scrunched his nose. "How's
that?" he asked. He patted his pocket, looking
for his glasses. "Here they are, Dad," said
Curie, lowering Artemis' glasses from his head
to his nose.

"Oh," Chief Thomas said. "I'll just let them tell you how they're both chips off the old block."

Nick and Curie looked at their dad and smiled.

THE END

ABOUT THE AUTHOR

Carole Marsh is an author and publisher who has written many works of fiction and non-fiction for young readers. She travels throughout the United States and around the world to research her books. In 1979 Carole Marsh was named Communicator of the Year for her corporate communications work with major national and international corporations.

Marsh is the founder and CEO of Gallopade International, established in 1979. Today, Gallopade International is widely recognized as a leading source of educational materials for every state and many countries. Marsh and Gallopade were recipients of the 2004 Teachers' Choice Award. Marsh has written more than 50 Carole Marsh Mysteries™. In 2007, she was named Georgia Author of the Year. Years ago, her children, Michele and Michael, were the original characters in her mystery books. Today, they continue the Carole Marsh Books tradition by working at Gallopade. By adding grandchildren Grant and Christina as new mystery characters, she has continued the tradition for a third generation.

Ms. Marsh welcomes correspondence from her readers. You can e-mail her at fanclub@gallopade.com, visit carolemarshmysteries.com, or write to her in care of Gallopade International, P.O. Box 2779, Peachtree City, Georgia, 30269 USA.

Book Club:
Talk About It!

1. Have you ever been camping and had to make a campfire? How did you start the fire safely? What was fun about having a campfire?

2. If you have been camping, what is your favorite food cooked on the fire?

3. What did Nick and Curie do to put out their campfire? What did Ralph and Tom do? What was wrong about what Ralph and Tom did?

4. Artemis's favorite animal is the horse. What is your favorite animal and why?

5. It's important to properly put out a campfire so you don't start a forest fire. What are some reasons you should not play with fire?

6. Artemis said, "It takes a brave person or a little bit crazy one to run into a fire." What does he mean by that statement?

7. Do you know what to do if there's a fire in your house? Talk about safety measures and possible quick escape routes with your class, teachers, and parents.

8. What part of the story was scarier for you—the fire or the rattlesnake?

9. Ralph and Tom were on a hitchhiking adventure. Do you think hitchhiking is a good idea or a bad idea? Why?

10. Artemis and the horses jumped off a high cliff! Are you afraid of heights?

Book Club:
Bring It to Life!

1. Write a fun poem or even a rap song about fire safety. Include common things like don't play with matches, stop, drop, and roll, put out a campfire completely, and have an escape route in your house in case of fire. Research other fire safety tips, too. Share your poem or song with other club members. Vote on your favorite!

2. Smokey Bear is very popular mascot for teaching about fire safety. First, look up the definition for "mascot." Then, write a story about spending a day with Smokey in Yellowstone National Park! Where would you go? What would you eat? Who would you talk to?

3. Horses LOVE sugar cubes! You can have fun with them, too! Get a box of sugar cubes and some glue and construct your own creation. Your book club group can make a whole town out of sugar! Sweeeeeet!

4. A Yin Yang is a symbol made of two
    pieces that complete a circle. The two
    pieces fit perfectly to show unity. You
    could say that a Yin Yang looks like a little
    puzzle. Glue colorful construction paper
    to cardboard and cut it into several
    pieces. Make your own puzzles and trade
    with your friends to see who can figure
    them out!

GLOSSARY

acronym: a word formed by the first letters of a group of words or phrases

aeronautical engineering: a kind of engineering that focuses on making machines to work outside of the earth's atmosphere

ecosystem: a collection of living things and the environment in which they live

evaporate: when moisture changes from liquid to gas in the air

flammable: any material that is easily set on fire

foliage: a grouping of leaves or brush

humble: not arrogant; modest

implicate: to reveal as being involved in a situation

incendiary: capable of causing fire

infringe: to violate, go against, or conflict with rules or laws

ingenious: cleverly inventive

mud slurry: a thin mixture of mud and water

thermal: relating to or associated with heat

Forest Fire Trivia

1. A controlled fire is one that is monitored by the fire department and allowed to burn to help maintain a healthy forest environment. It helps the ecosystem by allowing plants to regrow using ashes as a natural fertilizer.

2. Severe droughts create the perfect dry conditions for a forest fire.

3. In the summer of 1988, 700,000 acres of Yellowstone National Park were burned in a forest fire. The burned area was nearly one-third of the park.

4. If lightning strikes brush that is already dried out, a forest fire can quickly start. One percent of lightning strikes result in a fire.

5. During a forest fire, the animals will scatter to parts of the forest that are not burning.

6. Even campfires that have burned out can become reignited in the presence of oxygen if not doused with water and packed with dirt completely.

7. Dropping water on an area where a wildfire has started isn't always the best solution because the heat of the fire will evaporate the water before it has a chance to act.

8. Fire tornadoes are formed when two different air masses mix and cause the flames to travel with the air in a swirling motion.

9. In 1926, thousands of fire tornadoes appeared at the same time during an out-of-control wildfire in California.

10. Foscheck is sometimes known as red rain because it is dropped on fires from a helicopter, making it look like the sky is raining red.

Get to Know Smokey Bear!

1. Smokey Bear is the forest fire prevention symbol of the U.S. Forest Service.

2. Smokey Bear is such an important advertising symbol that he is protected by federal law!

3. Smokey Bear was named after "Smokey" Joe Martin, a brave firefighter who served for 47 years in the New York Fire Department in the first half of the 20th century.

4. The first poster featuring Smokey Bear was produced in 1944.

5. Smokey Bear was given his own zip code because he receives so much fan mail!

6. Even the U.S. Postal Service thinks a lot of Smokey Bear. He was the first individual animal to be honored on a postage stamp! The 20-cent stamp commemorated his 40th birthday in 1984.

Forest Fire Scavenger Hunt

Want to have some fun? Let's go on a scavenger hunt! See if you can find the items below related to the mystery. *(Teachers: You have permission to reproduce this page for your students.)*

1. _____ a bucket

2. _____ a shovel

3. _____ a stuffed bear

4. _____ a fire extinguisher

5. _____ a horseshoe

6. _____ a plastic bag

7. _____ some chewing gum

8. _____ a poncho

9. _____ a ticket stub

10. _____ a necklace or a chain

Forest Fire Pop Quiz

1. What is "dry lightning?"

2. What does longitude measure?

3. Why is Foscheck colored red?

4. What does a smokejumper do for a living?

5. Why was Artemis so concerned about the missing horses?

6. Why did Artemis' cell phone stop working?

7. What kind of hat was Ralph wearing when the kids spotted him?

8. What did Artemis name the horses he rescued?

TECH CONNECTs

Hey, Kids!
Visit www.carolemarshmysteries.com to:

Join the Carole Marsh Mysteries Fan Club!

Write one sensational sentence using all five
SAT words in the glossary!

Download a Forest Fire Word Search!

Take a Pop Quiz!

Download a Scavenger Hunt!

Read Ferocious Forest Fire Trivia!